For Aysha Daisy Waterfield – M. R.

For the McCalls, Jamie, Helen, Milly & Henry x – N. E.

PUFFIN BOOKS
Published by the Penguin Group: London, New York,
Australia, Canada, India, Ireland, New Zealand and South Africa
Penguin Books Ltd, Registered Offices: 80 Strand, London WC2R 0RL, England
puffinbooks.com
First published 2014
001

Made and printed in China
ISBN: 978–0–723–29364–4

Goodnight Santa

Michelle Robinson

Illustrated by **Nick East**

PUFFIN

It's Christmas Eve!
Hop on the sled.
It's time we took you
home to bed.

Goodnight snowman.

Goodnight choir.

Goodnight stockings by the fire.

to Santa x

Goodnight tree

and mistletoe...

Santa's coming! Ho ho ho!

Sparkling snowflakes swirl and swish.
Close your eyes and make a wish . . .

Through the snowdrifts, hand in hand.

Goodnight winter wonderland.

picking presents from the shelves!

Goodnight workshop.
Goodnight toys.
Where's that list
of girls and boys?

Come on, reindeer.
Time to go . . .

Here comes Santa! Ho ho ho!

Look! It's Santa and his elves

The world below is frosty white.

There's magic in the air tonight!

Reindeer, rooftops, cosy fires.

Sacks and snowmen, trees and

choirs.

Gifts of every
shape
and size.

Jingling
bells
and
starry skies.

Two more stockings

still to go . . .

Goodnight Santa! Ho ho ho!